All by Myself

Richard Brown

Illustrated by Gill Scriven

CAMBRIDGE
UNIVERSITY PRESS

When I was two, I liked to go on the
little slide. But I really wanted to go on
the big slide.

One day, I climbed up to the top of
the big slide.

I was frightened up there. It was much
too high.

I screamed and screamed.

After that, I was frightened of anywhere
that was high.
I had to be carried up the stairs in buses.

I had to be carried over bridges.
I always shut my eyes.

Much later, when I was five, I learnt
to swim. I learnt to jump from the side of
the pool, too.

But I really wanted to learn to jump from the diving-board. Mum said that I could try.

The first time I stood on the diving-board,
it felt too high. I was very frightened.

But I said to myself, "I *will* do it."
I took a big step along the diving-board.

The next time, I took two big steps.
Then three. I still felt frightened, but I really
wanted to do it.

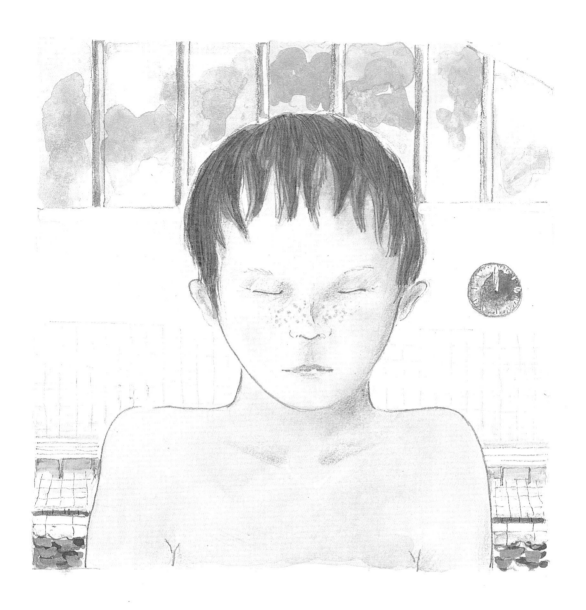

At last, I reached the end of the
diving-board.

I shut my eyes.

I bent my legs, and I was about to jump,

but it still felt too high. I couldn't quite do it.
"I *will* do it," I said to myself.

Then, I took a deep breath and . . .

. . . SPLASH! I'd done it.
And I'd done it all by myself.